THE HEROES OF OLYMPUS

BOOK TWO

THE SON OF NEPTUNE

THE GRAPHIC NOVEL

by

RICK RIORDAN

Adapted by
ROBERT VENDITTI

Art by
ANTOINE DODÉ

Color by
ORPHEUS COLLAR

Lettering by
CHRIS DICKEY

Gift of the Friends of
the Pleasant Hill Library

DISNEP · HYPERION
Los Angeles   New York

Adapted from the novel
The Heroes of Olympus, Book Two: *The Son of Neptune*

Text copyright © 2017 by Rick Riordan
Illustrations copyright © 2017 Disney Enterprises, Inc.

All rights reserved. Published by Disney • Hyperion, an imprint of Buena Vista Books, Inc.
No part of this book may be reproduced or transmitted in any form or by any means,
electronic or mechanical, including photocopying, recording, or by any information
storage and retrieval system, without written permission from the publisher. For information
address Disney • Hyperion, 77 West 66th Street, New York, New York 10023.

First Edition, February 2017
5 7 9 11 12 10 8 6

FAC-038091-21104
Printed in the United States of America

Text is set in Minion Pro and Lithos from Fontspring
Designed by Jim Titus

Library of Congress Cataloging-in-Publication Control Number: 2015031231

Library of Congress Cataloging-in-Publication Data

Names: Venditti, Robert, author. | Riordan, Rick. Son of Neptune. | Disney
Enterprises (1996-)
Title: The son of Neptune : the graphic novel / by Rick Riordan ; adapted by
Robert Venditti ; illustrations Disney Enterprises, Inc.
Description: First edition. | New York : Disney/Hyperion, [2016] | Series:
The heroes of Olympus : book 2 | Summary: Demigod Percy Jackson, still
with no memory, and his new friends from Camp Jupiter, Hazel and Frank, go
on a quest to free Death, but their bigger task is to unite the Greek and
Roman camps so that the Prophecy of Seven can be fulfilled.
Identifiers: LCCN 2015031231 | ISBN 9781484716212 (hardcover) | ISBN
9781484723036 (pbk.)
Subjects: LCSH: Mythology, Roman—Juvenile fiction. | Mythology,
Greek—Juvenile fiction. | Graphic novels. | CYAC: Graphic novels. |
Mythology, Roman—Fiction. | Mythology, Greek—Fiction. | Camps—Fiction.
| Hera (Greek deity)—Fiction. | Gaia (Greek deity)—Fiction. |
Monsters—Fiction. | Prophecies—Fiction. | Riordan, Rick. Son of
Neptune—Adaptations.
Classification: LCC PZ7.7.V48 So 2016 | DDC 741.5973—dc23
LC record available at https://lccn.loc.gov/2015031231

ISBN (hardcover) 978-1-4847-1621-2
ISBN (paperback) 978-1-4847-2303-6

Reinforced binding
Follow @ReadRiordan and visit
www.DisneyBooks.com

SUSTAINABLE
FORESTRY
INITIATIVE
Certified Sourcing
www.sfiprogram.org
SFI-00993
Logo Applies to Text Stock Only

LEAVE IT TO FRANK AND HAZEL TO BRING SOMEONE LIKE *HIM* TO CAMP.

YEAH. LET HIM JOIN THE *FIFTH COHORT. GREEKS* AND *GEEKS.*

WHAT THE--?!

SORRY. I...UH...DIDN'T SEE YOU THERE.

GRAECUS!

GRAECUS! GRAECUS!

YIPE! YIPE!

AM I SEEING THINGS, OR IS THAT A *GHOST*?

THEY'RE CALLED *"LARES."* HOUSE GODS. THEY'RE KIND OF LIKE MASCOTS. MOSTLY THEY'RE HARMLESS. I'VE NEVER SEEN ONE SO *AGITATED.*

GO TAKE AN INVENTORY OF THE ARMORY, FRANK. I'LL SEND FOR YOU IF YOU'RE NEEDED.

BUT, REYNA, I THOUGHT I'D--

I REMIND YOU, YOU'RE STILL ON *PROBATIO.* YOU'VE CAUSED YOURSELF ENOUGH *TROUBLE* THIS WEEK.

ALL RIGHT. SEE YOU LATER, HAZEL.

PERCY, THANKS FOR... YOU KNOW. HELPING ME AT THE RIVER.

DON'T MENTION IT.

YOU COULD'VE BEEN NICER TO FRANK. WITHOUT HIM AND HAZEL, ME AND THE *BAG-LADY* GODDESS WOULDN'T HAVE MADE IT HERE.

WHICH MAY NOT BE *GOOD.* WHAT THAT *LAR* SAID. *"GRAECUS."*

IT MEANS *"GREEK"* IN LATIN.

AND I'M REYNA AVILA RAMIREZ-ARELLANO, *PRAETOR* OF THE *TWELFTH LEGION.* "NICE" ISN'T PART OF MY JOB DESCRIPTION.

FOLLOW ME.

SHE TAUGHT ME ABOUT GODS AND DEMIGODS AND MONSTERS.

THEN SHE SENT ME SOUTH. SHE SAID IF I SURVIVED MY JOURNEY, I'D FIND A NEW HOME AND REGAIN MY MEMORY.

I REALLY HOPE THIS IS THE PLACE SHE WAS TALKING ABOUT.

BECAUSE NOT HAVING A MEMORY *STINKS*.

WHAT YOU'RE DESCRIBING IS NORMAL FOR A DEMIGOD. BUT WE USUALLY MAKE OUR WAY TO CAMP AT A MUCH YOUNGER AGE.

IT'S *RARE* THAT ONE OF US LASTS SO LONG ON OUR OWN. DO YOU HAVE ANY POSSESSIONS THAT MIGHT OFFER CLUES?

I'VE GOT THIS BEAD NECKLACE--

--BUT I HAVE NO IDEA WHAT THE SYMBOLS MEAN.

AND I HAVE A *PEN* THAT TURNS INTO A *BRONZE SWORD*.

I AM *NOT* MAKING THAT UP.

BRONZE? WE FIGHT MONSTERS WITH *IMPERIAL GOLD*.

IT'S CURIOUS YOU DON'T BEAR THE MARK OF THE LEGION, EITHER.

ONCE A MEMBER OF THE LEGION IS MARKED, THE MARKINGS CAN'T BE REMOVED.

SPQR

PERCY, IF YOU SURVIVED AS A LONER ALL THIS TIME, MAYBE YOU'VE SEEN *JASON*.

HAVE YOU EVER MET A DEMIGOD LIKE US BEFORE?

A KID IN A PURPLE SHIRT, WITH MARKS ON HIS ARM?

I HAVEN'T SEEN *ANYONE* LIKE YOU GUYS BEFORE. WHO'S JASON?

HE IS...HE *WAS* MY COLLEAGUE. THE LEGION NORMALLY HAS TWO ELECTED PRAETORS.

JASON GRACE, SON OF *JUPITER*, WAS OUR OTHER PRAETOR UNTIL HE DISAPPEARED LAST OCTOBER.

THAT'S *EIGHT MONTHS*. YOU HAVEN'T REPLACED HIM?

ELECTIONS ONLY HAPPEN TWO WAYS: EITHER SOMEONE IS RAISED ON THEIR SHIELD AFTER A MAJOR SUCCESS IN BATTLE--

--OR WE HOLD A BALLOT ON THE EVENING OF JUNE TWENTY-FOURTH, AT THE FEAST OF FORTUNE. THAT'S IN FIVE DAYS.

THE FEAST OF FORTUNE...

THE GORGONS MENTIONED THAT. JUNO, TOO.

THEY SAID CAMP WOULD BE *ATTACKED* ON THAT DAY.

SOMETHING ABOUT A BIG BAD GODDESS NAMED *GAEA*, AN ARMY, AND DEATH BEING UNLEASHED. YOU'RE TELLING ME THAT'S THIS *WEEK*?

YOU WILL SAY *NOTHING* ABOUT THAT OUTSIDE THIS ROOM. UNDERSTAND?

I'LL NOT HAVE YOU SPREADING MORE *PANIC* THROUGH THE CAMP.

SO IT'S *TRUE*. CAN WE STOP IT?

WE'VE TALKED ENOUGH FOR NOW.

HAZEL, TAKE HIM TO TEMPLE HILL.

YES, REYNA.

GOOD LUCK WITH THE *AUGURY*, PERCY JACKSON. PERHAPS WE CAN COMPARE MORE NOTES LATER--

YOU MEAN THIS? ONCE UPON A TIME, AUGURS USED TO READ THE WILL OF THE GODS BY EXAMINING ANIMAL GUTS. NOWADAYS WE USE *STUFFED TOYS.*

NOT AS DRAMATIC AS THE OLD WAYS.

ALSO NOT AS DIFFICULT TO CLEAN UP.

DON'T YOU HAVE...I DON'T KNOW, AN *ORACLE* OR SOMETHING?

AN ORACLE! HOW QUAINT!

WE'RE FRESH OUT OF ORACLES.

NOW, IF WE'D GONE QUESTING FOR THE *SIBYLLINE BOOKS* LIKE I RECOMMENDED, THAT'D MAKE MY LIFE MUCH EASIER.

BOOKS OF PROPHECY. ANCIENT ROMANS USED TO CONSULT THEM WHEN DISASTERS HAPPENED. MOST PEOPLE BELIEVE THEY BURNED UP WHEN ROME FELL.

OCTAVIAN IS KIND OF *OBSESSED* WITH THEM.

GOTCHA.

THE BOOKS DID *NOT* BURN. I'M CERTAIN OF IT. UNFORTUNATELY, OUR SOLE PRAETOR WON'T AUTHORIZE A QUEST TO LOOK FOR THEM.

ALL WE HAVE ARE A FEW SCRAPS WITH MYSTERIOUS PREDICTIONS.

-*ahem*-
"SEVEN HALF-BLOODS SHALL ANSWER THE CALL. TO STORM OR FIRE THE WORLD MUST FALL--"

"--AN OATH TO KEEP WITH A FINAL BREATH, AND FOES BEAR ARMS TO THE DOORS OF DEATH."

PERCY? YOU DON'T LOOK SO GOOD.

IT'S JUST...I KNOW THAT ONE. IT'S *IMPORTANT*. BUT I CAN'T REMEMBER WHY.

OF COURSE IT'S IMPORTANT. WE CALL IT THE *PROPHECY OF SEVEN*, BUT IT'S SEVERAL THOUSAND YEARS OLD.

WE DON'T KNOW WHAT IT MEANS. EVERY TIME SOMEONE TRIES TO INTERPRET IT, BAD STUFF HAPPENS. ASK *HAZEL*.

JUST READ THE AUGURY FOR PERCY, *ALL RIGHT*, OCTAVIAN?

CAN HE JOIN THE LEGION, OR NOT? WE NEED TO KNOW BEFORE THE *WAR GAMES*.

PATIENCE, PATIENCE. GIMME A SEC...

AH. A BEAUTIFUL SPECIMEN.

HMMM...

SHRRRIP

YEP. HE'S GOOD TO GO. TELL REYNA THAT I APPROVE.

WELCOME TO THE TWELFTH, SON OF NEPTUNE.

GREAT. COME ON, PERCY.

WE CAME ALL THE WAY TO TEMPLE HILL FOR *THAT*?

OH, HAZEL? WHEN THE ELECTIONS FOR *NEW PRAETOR* COME UP ON THE FEAST OF FORTUNE...

...I HOPE YOU'LL REMEMBER TO GIVE ME YOUR VOTE.

IF I'M ELECTED, I'LL DO EVERYTHING IN MY POWER TO HELP YOU IN THE EVENT THOSE AWFUL *RUMORS* ABOUT YOU CONTINUE TO CIRCULATE.

OR--GODS FORBID--SHOULD THEY TURN OUT TO BE *TRUE*.

I'LL THINK ABOUT IT.

THAT'S ALL I CAN ASK.

NOW, I'M BACK TO CONSULTING THE GODS IN REGARDS TO OUR LOST, *BELOVED* PRAETOR, JASON.

AND, HAZEL?

"SAY HI TO YOUR **BROTHER** FOR ME."

NICO? WHAT ARE YOU DOING HERE?

GOOD TO SEE YOU, TOO, SIS--

OH.

THIS IS PERCY JACKSON. HE JUST ARRIVED AT CAMP TODAY.

FLYING GORGONS? BIG HANDS MADE OUT OF WATER? THAT WAS ME.

WHAT'S YOUR NAME AGAIN?

NICO.

NICO DI ANGELO.

UM...PERCY? WHY DON'T YOU GO FIND FRANK. TELL HIM OCTAVIAN GAVE YOU APPROVAL TO JOIN THE LEGION.

HE'LL HELP YOU GET CLEANED UP BEFORE EVENING MUSTER.

SURE. SEE YOU LATER, HAZEL. AND GOOD TO MEET YOU, NICO. I'LL SEE YOU AROUND.

I'VE **ZERO** DOUBT.

YOU **RECOGNIZE** HIM, DON'T YOU? YOU'VE MET HIM BEFORE.

PERCY JACKSON.

HAZEL, I HAVE TO BE CAREFUL WHAT I SAY. SOME SECRETS NEED TO **STAY** SECRET. IMPORTANT THINGS ARE AT WORK HERE.

IS HE... DANGEROUS?

VERY. BUT ONLY TO HIS ENEMIES.

YOU CAN TRUST HIM. HE'S ONE OF THE GOOD ONES.

THAT MUCH I CAN PROMISE YOU.

POP!

LOOK AT THE SIZE OF *THAT* ONE.

DON'T TOUCH IT!

RELAX. IT'S ME, REMEMBER? WE'RE BOTH HALF-BLOOD KIDS OF *PLUTO*.

WE REPRESENT HIS TWO SPHERES OF CONTROL. I'M *DEATH*, AND YOU'RE *RICHES*.

WE HAVE NOTHING TO FEAR FROM EACH OTHER.

ALL THE SAME, I'LL GET RID OF THIS SOMEWHERE NO ONE WILL FIND IT.

AND IF YOU CAN, TRY NOT TO MAKE TOO MANY OF THESE. YOU KNOW WHAT HAPPENS WHEN PEOPLE PICK THEM UP. THE MORE *VALUABLE* THEY ARE, THE *DEADLIER*...

CRASH

AAAA!

HUSH NOW, CHILD. YOU'LL BE ALL RIGHT.

EVERYTHING WILL BE ALL RIGHT.

~sniff~ DADDY?

YOU LEAVE HER BE! JUST GO!

I'VE SAID ALL I CAN.

THE CHOICE IS YOURS.

FWOOF

DADDY?

HAZEL! PACK YOUR THINGS! WE'RE MOVING.

TONIGHT!

DO YOU HEAR ME, YOUNG LADY?

HAZEL!

HAZEL!

UHNNNN...

S-SORRY. I DID IT AGAIN, DIDN'T I?

DON'T BE. WHERE WERE YOU THIS TIME?

MY MOTHER'S APARTMENT. THE DAY WE MOVED.

FLASHBACKS. IT'S A SIDE EFFECT FROM YOUR TIME IN THE UNDERWORLD. IT HAS TO BE.

YOU HAVE TO WORK ON CONTROLLING THEM. IF SOMETHING LIKE THAT HAPPENS WHILE YOU'RE IN COMBAT...

I CAN'T GO NORTH AGAIN, NICO. I CAN'T GO BACK TO WHERE IT HAPPENED.

YOU'LL GO WHERE THE QUEST TAKES YOU. AND YOU'LL HAVE FRIENDS THIS TIME. PERCY IS A GOOD GUY TO HAVE IN YOUR CORNER. YOU'LL SEE.

NOW, LET'S GET BACK TO THE OTHERS.

I HAVE A FEELING TONIGHT'S WAR GAMES ARE GOING TO BE INTERESTING.

HI.

UNFORTUNATELY, PERCY ARRIVED WITH NO LETTER OF *RECOMMENDATION* FROM A FORMER LEGIONNAIRE. WHO WILL STAND FOR HIM?

I WILL!

I WILL STAND FOR PERCY JACKSON!

VERY WELL.

CENTURIONS, YOU AND YOUR COHORTS HAVE *ONE HOUR* BEFORE WE CONVENE FOR WAR GAMES ON THE FIELD OF MARS.

THE FIRST AND SECOND COHORTS WILL DEFEND. THE THIRD, FOURTH, AND FIFTH WILL ATTACK.

GOOD LUCK WITH THE *FIFTH*, PERCY.

"YOU'LL NEED IT."

SO THIS TABLET MEANS I'M IN?

I'LL DO MY BEST.

NOT EXACTLY. YOU'RE ON *PROBATIO*, LIKE FRANK. AFTER A YEAR-- OR IF YOU PERFORM AN ACT OF VALOR--YOU'LL BE A FULL MEMBER OF THE TWELFTH.

SINCE I STOOD FOR YOU, YOU'RE MY RESPONSIBILITY. IT'S MY JOB TO MAKE SURE YOU DON'T *DISGRACE* THE LEGION.

I HOPE SO. MAKE TOO BIG A MISTAKE, AND I'LL GET KILLED ALONG WITH YOU.

SAY WHAT?

WELCOME TO THE *PERCY*, PARTY!

I MEAN PARTY, PERCY. WHATEVER.

DON'T MIND DAKOTA. HE'S *BACCHUS'S* KID. INSTEAD OF WINE, HE'S HOOKED ON KOOL-AID. HE MIXES IT WITH *THREE TIMES* THE SUGAR. NOT GOOD FOR HIS ADHD.

HE'S ALL RIGHT, THOUGH. HE STOOD UP FOR HAZEL, AFTER ALL.

SHICF

HAZEL! MY FAVORITE GIRL!

PERCY, THIS IS DON. HE'S ONE OF THE FAUNS.

YOU GONNA EAT THAT PLATE, NEW KID?

THE SEE-THROUGH ONE IS *VITELLIUS*, HOUSE *GHOST* OF THE FIFTH COHORT.

UNFORTUNATELY.

BACK IN CAESAR'S DAY--

--THAT'S *JULIUS* CAESAR, MIND YOU--

--THE FIFTH WAS THE *PRIDE* OF ROME.

NOW? *DISGRACEFUL!*

-sniff-
-sniff-

CAN I HELP YOU?

MAN, YOU'VE GOT AN *EMPATHY LINK* ON YOU. WHO YOU BEEN HANGING WITH?

I HAVE NO IDEA.

DAKOTA, YOU'RE CENTURION OF THE FIFTH COHORT.

DON'T YOU THINK WE SHOULD USE THIS TIME TO *STRATEGIZE* FOR THE WAR GAMES?

FINE. LET'S GO.

-sigh-

I NEED A *REFILL* ANYWAY.

OKAY, SO TELL ME. WHY'S IT SO BAD TO BE IN THE FIFTH COHORT? YOU GUYS SEEM PRETTY GREAT.

IT'S WHERE THEY PUT ALL THE *MISFITS*. TAKE ME. ROMAN FIGHTING IS DONE ON FOOT, BUT MY BIG DREAM IS TO RIDE *CAVALRY*.

AND I WANT TO BE AN *ARCHER*. ROMANS AREN'T KEEN ON THAT, EITHER. PLUS, THEY SAY I'M TOO *BIG* AND *BULKY*.

I KEEP HOPING APOLLO WILL CLAIM ME AS HIS SON, BUT THE APOLLO KIDS TELL ME *FAT CHANCE*.

BUT THE *REAL* PROBLEM GOES BACK A LOT FARTHER.

WAY BEFORE OUR TIME HERE.

SEE THE EMPTY POLE AMONG THE OTHER STANDARDS?

"THERE'S SUPPOSED TO BE A *GOLD EAGLE* THERE. IT'S THE SYMBOL OF THE WHOLE CAMP."

"THEY SAY IT WAS CHARGED WITH POWER FROM *JUPITER* HIMSELF. POWER TO PROTECT US IN BATTLE AND MAKE OUR ENEMIES AFRAID."

BUT IT'S GONE NOW.

BECAUSE OF THE FIFTH?

THAT PROPHECY YOU HEARD IN THE TEMPLE ABOUT THE DOORS OF DEATH?

OUR OLD SENIOR PRAETOR-- BEFORE REYNA--HIS NAME WAS MICHAEL VARUS.

HE WENT TO *ALASKA* TO FIGURE OUT THE PROPHECY.

THE AUGURIES WARNED HIM IT WASN'T TIME, BUT HE THOUGHT IT'D BRING *HONOR* TO THE LEGION.

LET'S JUST SAY IT *DIDN'T*. WE LOST A LOT OF CAMPERS.

MOST OF THE LEGION'S IMPERIAL GOLD WEAPONS WERE TAKEN, ALONG WITH THE EAGLE.

MICHAEL WAS FROM THE *FIFTH*, SO...

WE'VE BEEN OUTCASTS EVER SINCE. EVERYONE THINKS WE'RE *CURSED*. JASON? HE WAS FROM THE FIFTH, TOO. NOW HE'S DISAPPEARED.

MEANWHILE, WITHOUT THE EAGLE, THE CAMP HAS BEEN GETTING WEAKER.

MONSTERS ARE ATTACKING US MORE OFTEN.

SO, YOU KNOW, THAT'S WHAT YOU'VE GOTTEN YOURSELF INTO.

I'LL TAKE BEING WITH YOU GUYS OVER GETTING CHASED THROUGH THE WILDERNESS BY MONSTERS ANY DAY.

BESIDES, I GET THE FEELING THIS ISN'T THE FIRST TIME I'VE BEEN AN *UNDERDOG*.

MAYBE TOGETHER WE CAN TURN THINGS AROUND.

THAT'S THE SPIRIT. NOW LET'S GET TO THE WAR GAMES AND SEE IF WE CAN RACK UP OUR *THIRTEENTH* LOSS IN A *ROW*.

"IT IS TIME YOU FOUND YOURS."

HOPING A LITTLE *GORGON'S BLOOD* WILL HELP WITH YOUR *STICK* PROBLEM, EH?

WHAT? THIS IS JUST A PIECE OF *SCRAP WOOD* I PICKED UP! AND I DON'T HAVE ANY *GORGON'S BLOOD!*

DON'T TAKE *ME* FOR A FOOL, ZHANG!

HEY!

I SAW YOU GRAB THE VIALS AFTER PERCY KILLED THE GORGONS. THE SPOILS ARE *HIS* BY RIGHT. BUT YOU UNDERSTAND THEIR WORTH.

BLOOD FROM THE RIGHT SIDE OF A GORGON CAN CURE *ANYTHING.*

MAYBE EVEN *BREAK* YOUR *BOND* TO THE STICK.

BUT BLOOD FROM THE *LEFT* SIDE-- *INSTANTANEOUS* DEATH!

HOW TO TELL WHICH IS WHICH...

MIND YOUR OWN *BUSINESS,* VITELLIUS. I'M JUST...HOLDING THESE FOR PERCY. HE DOESN'T KNOW YET ABOUT THE *TROPHIES* MONSTERS LEAVE BEHIND AFTER THEY'RE KILLED.

YOU MIND *YOUR* BUSINESS, ZHANG! STICKS AND VIALS. *FIE!*

IN THE *PUNIC WARS,* A ROMAN THOUGHT ONLY OF *GUTTING* HIS ENEMY WITH SPEAR AND SWORD LIKE A *CIVILIZED* MAN!

THE FIRST AND SECOND COHORTS DID A SOLID JOB TODAY.

WAIT. YOU'RE TELLING ME THEY BUILT THAT FORTRESS *TODAY*?

LEGIONNAIRES ARE TRAINED TO BUILD.

IF WE HAD TO, WE COULD TAKE DOWN THE *ENTIRE CAMP* AND REBUILD IT SOMEPLACE ELSE.

IT'D TAKE A COUPLE DAYS, BUT WE COULD DO IT.

OH, WELL. IT'LL ALL BE OVER QUICK FOR US ANYWAY. THE REST OF THE FIFTH IS BEING SENT IN FIRST TO "SOFTEN THE DEFENSES." WE'LL BE *FODDER*, LIKE ALWAYS.

THEY WENT ALL-OUT. GUARD TOWERS, SCORPION BALLISTAE...

A *WATER CANNON*...

FRANK?

...I THINK I...

YEP. I DO. DEFINITELY.

I HAVE A *PLAN*.

CHARGE!

THERE'S AN *ELEPHANT?*

HANNIBAL. DON'T FEED HIM PEANUTS. THEY GIVE HIM INDIGESTION.

GREAT. WE DO ALL THE *WORK,* AND THE THIRD AND FOURTH WILL CLAIM THE *GLORY.*

NO WAY. WE EARNED THOSE BANNERS.

THIS IS *OUR* VICTORY.

CONGRATULATIONS, FRANK. YOU'LL GET THE MURAL CROWN FOR THIS. YOU DID REALLY GREAT.

WE DID GREAT.

NOT BAD FOR *GREEKS* AND *GEEKS*.

SOMEBODY HELP!

GWEN'S HURT BAD!

NO!

SHE'S... GONE.

THIS SWORD...

...IT BELONGS TO SOMEONE FROM THE *FIRST*.

THERE WILL BE A **THOROUGH** INVESTIGATION INTO THIS.

WHOEVER DID THIS, YOU COST THE LEGION A GOOD CENTURION.

HONORABLE DEATH IS ONE THING. BUT STABBING SOMEONE FROM **BEHIND** IS A COWARD'S STROKE.

INVESTIGATION? I KNOW JUST WHERE TO START. I SEE **YOU** DON'T HAVE A SWORD, OCTAVIAN.

WHAT OF IT, ZHANG? THERE WAS A **BATTLE**, IN CASE YOU HAVEN'T HEARD. SWORDS GET LOST IN BATTLE.

-=GASP=-

SH-UK

OW.

GWEN? YOU'RE... YOU WERE...

I THINK I WAS DREAMING.

THERE WAS A RIVER AND A MAN ASKING FOR A COIN. I TURNED AROUND, AND THERE WAS AN **EXIT DOOR** OPEN. SO I JUST LEFT.

THAT'S ALL I REMEMBER.

THANATOS HAS BEEN CHAINED. THE DOORS OF DEATH HAVE BEEN FORCED OPEN.

NO ONE IS POLICING THEM. GAEA'S GIANTS ARE MUSTERING ARMIES OF MONSTERS YOU WILL *NEVER* BE ABLE TO DEFEAT.

ALMIGHTY, MAGNIFICENT LORD MARS, IF THERE'S NO DEATH...THAT MEANS *WE* CAN'T DIE EITHER, RIGHT? ISN'T THAT A *GOOD* THING?

DON'T BE AN *IDIOT!*

ENDLESS *CARNAGE* AS FOES RISE AGAIN AND AGAIN? WHAT GOOD IS WAR, IF YOU CAN'T *WIN* IT?

UNLESS DEATH IS UNLEASHED AND RETURNED TO HIS DUTIES BY THE FEAST OF FORTUNE, YOU WILL BE *OVERRUN*.

ONLY THANATOS CAN REVERSE THE TIDE.

I ORDER A *QUEST*. THREE OF YOU WILL GO *NORTH* TO THE LAND BEYOND THE GODS.

YOU WILL FREE THANATOS AND *THWART* THE GIANTS' PLANS.

BEWARE GAEA!

BEWARE HER SON, THE *ELDEST* GIANT!

YOU, C'MERE.

ME?

YEAH, YOU. YOU'RE ZHANG, RIGHT?

FRANK ZHANG, SON OF EMILY.

UM, YEAH.

I'M YOUR *DAD*. NICE JOB BEING FIRST OVER THE WALL IN THE BATTLE. YOU GOT YOUR OLD MAN'S SPIRIT.

YOU'RE GONNA LEAD THIS QUEST.

TAKE THE *WATER BOY* WITH YOU. HE'LL LEARN TO RESPECT MARS ON THIS TRIP, OR *DIE* TRYING.

YOU GET IN A *PINCH*, USE THIS SPEAR. JUST JAM IT IN THE GROUND AND GET OUT OF THE WAY.

ONLY THREE CHARGES, SO USE IT WISELY.

WAIT! YOU'RE--

FWOOSH

AVE!

FRANK ZHANG!

SON OF MARS!

WELL, AT LEAST NOW YOU KNOW WHO YOUR *DAD* IS...

YEAH.

PERFECT.

"I AWAIT YOU ATOP THE *ICE*."

WHAT'S WITH THE CRAZY *DREAMS*?

WHO'S *ALCYONEUS*...?

PERCY?

YOU READY FOR THE SENATE MEETING?

RIGHT... THE MEETING. WHY ARE WE GOING TO THAT, ANYWAY?

BECAUSE... YOU KNOW. THE QUEST.

IT'S *OUR* QUEST, SO WE HAVE TO BE IN ON THE DISCUSSION. HAZEL, ME, AND YOU.

I MEAN, IF YOU'RE STILL GOING.

DON'T BRING ANY WEAPONS WITH YOU. *TERMINUS*, THE GOD OF BOUNDARIES? HE PROTECTS THE BORDERS OF THE CITY. HE'S KIND OF A *STICKLER* FOR RULES.

HE'S ALSO A *STATUE*, BUT IT'S WEIRD BECAUSE HE--

YEAH, SURE. LET'S JUST GET READY.

WE'RE NOT GATHERED IN OUR SENATE HOUSE TO VOTE ON THE QUEST ITSELF. IT HAS BEEN ISSUED BY *MARS ULTOR*, PATRON OF ROME.

WE WILL OBEY HIS WISHES.

NOR ARE WE TO DEBATE THE CHOICE OF COMPANIONS.

FRANK HAS THE RIGHT TO MAKE HIS OWN SELECTIONS... EVEN IF THEY ARE BOTH FROM THE FIFTH COHORT.

HOWEVER, THERE ARE *RULES*. CHIEF AMONG THEM, A QUEST MUST BE LED BY A SOLDIER OF *CENTURION* RANK OR HIGHER.

FRANK ZHANG IS STILL ON *PROBATIO*, BUT MARS ULTOR HAS *DECLARED* THAT FRANK BE THE LEADER OF THIS QUEST. BEARING THAT IN MIND--

--*FRANK ZHANG*, COME FORWARD.

MARS SAID TO GO TO THE LAND BEYOND THE GODS. THAT MEANS *ALASKA*.

-*gasp*-

THAT'S CRAZY! ALASKA IS *CURSED*!

IT'S CALLED THE LAND BEYOND THE GODS FOR A REASON. IT'S SO FAR NORTH, THE GODS HAVE NO POWER THERE. IT'S *SWARMING* WITH MONSTERS!

LOOK, I KNOW I'M NEW HERE, BUT THIS SEEMS OBVIOUS TO ME.

THE FIFTH LED THE EXPEDITION WHERE YOU LOST YOUR EAGLE.

THE GIANT MARS IS SENDING US AFTER--HE BEAT THE FIFTH ONCE, AND NOW HE'S ADDED A *DEATH GOD* TO HIS TROPHY CASE.

IT'S UP TO THE FIFTH TO BEAT HIM AND GET IT ALL BACK.

SAY YOU'RE RIGHT. ALASKA IS ONLY, LIKE, THE *BIGGEST* STATE IN THE COUNTRY.

THE FEAST OF FORTUNE IS IN *FOUR DAYS*.

DO YOU KNOW WHERE TO LOOK? DO YOU EVEN KNOW THIS GIANT'S *NAME*?

I DON'T KNOW EXACTLY WHERE TO LOOK. BUT HIS NAME IS *ALCYONEUS*.

HOW DO *YOU* KNOW SO MUCH ABOUT OUR *ENEMY*, HAZEL?

EACH GIANT WAS BRED TO OPPOSE A PARTICULAR GOD. ALCYONEUS IS THE ELDEST.

HE'S *PLUTO'S* OPPOSITE. HE'S LIKELIEST TO MAKE A PLAY AT DEATH.

AS CHILDREN OF PLUTO, IT'S HAZEL'S AND MY JOB TO KNOW THIS STUFF.

JUST AS WE KNOW THAT ALCYONEUS HAS A *SPECIAL POWER*-- HE CAN'T BE KILLED IN HIS HOME TERRITORY.

THAT'S WHY THE 1980S EXPEDITION FAILED.

I'M AFRAID OCTAVIAN IS RIGHT. THERE ISN'T MUCH TIME.

HOW DO YOU INTEND TO GET TO ALASKA AND FREE THANATOS IN JUST FOUR DAYS?

ESPECIALLY IF YOU DON'T KNOW ALCYONEUS'S EXACT LOCATION?

I'M THE SON OF *NEPTUNE*. SO GIVE ME A BOAT.

AFTER THAT... WE IMPROVISE.

~*sigh*~ TIME IS SHORT. THAT WILL HAVE TO DO.

SENATORS, I CALL THE VOTE.

ALL IN FAVOR OF CENTURION FRANK ZHANG, HAZEL LEVESQUE, AND PERCY JACKSON EMBARKING ON THIS QUEST, RAISE A HAND.

THEN THE MATTER IS DECIDED. MAKE PREPARATIONS AT ONCE.

PERCY JACKSON, YOU WILL JOIN ME IN THE *PRINCIPIA*, WHERE I WILL SPEAK TO YOU FURTHER.

ALONE.

SOMETHING ABOUT THAT PLACE... THE MOUNTAIN LOOKS FAMILIAR.

I THINK I WENT THERE LOOKING FOR MY GIRLFRIEND. YEAH... I REMEMBER. HER NAME IS *ANNABETH*.

MOUNT TAM. KIDS AT CAMP ARE ALWAYS TALKING ABOUT IT. A BIG BATTLE HAPPENED THERE AT THE OLD TITAN BASE.

THE LEGION DESTROYED THE ENEMY'S PALACE AND ABOUT A MILLION MONSTERS. JASON WENT HAND-TO-HAND AGAINST THE TITAN *KRIOS* HIMSELF.

THAT WAS BACK IN AUGUST, BEFORE HAZEL AND I GOT TO CAMP.

HAZEL? ARE YOU GETTING SEASICK?

MWUUH

WMMP

OH, NO...

YOUR CYCLOPES MOVE *INEXCUSABLY SLOWLY,* MA GASKET!

MY BROTHER, *ALCYONEUS,* WANTS US AT CAMP JUPITER IN *FOUR DAYS'* TIME!

YOU HEAR THAT, *SLOWPOKES*?! FOUR DAYS!

AW, BUT WE'RE *HUNGRY,* MA!

YOU CAN EAT THE *CAMPERS* WHEN WE GET THERE!

NOW *MOVE* IT!

SNIFF SNIFF

I SMELL GOD.

PERHAPS THE CONVENIENCE STORE? WE COULD ALSO GET SOME *SNACKS*...

NICE TRY, GASKET.

BUT WE HAVE *LARGER* BATTLES TO WAGE.

BUT I'LL LEAVE THESE *SENTRIES* AS A GIFT.

HSSS

HSSS

KEEP AN EYE OUT.

POLYBOTES'S *HAIR SNAKES* ARE LURKING SOMEWHERE.

PERCY? YOU LOOK SICK.

...POLYBOTES.

I NEED TO SIT DOWN.

LET'S GET HIM INSIDE. I DON'T LIKE IT OUT HERE.

"WE HAVE *A LOT* TO TALK ABOUT."

I CAN IMAGINE HOW YOU MUST FEEL, FRANK. THAT HALF-BURNT STICK FEELING *HEAVIER* IN YOUR POCKET EVERY DAY.

HOW DO YOU--?

I WAS JUNO'S MESSENGER FOR AGES. THAT'S WHY I ALSO KNOW SHE GAVE YOU A REPRIEVE.

SHE WANTS YOU TO SERVE IN HER PLAN.

IF SHE HADN'T APPEARED THAT DAY WHEN YOU WERE A BABY AND WARNED YOUR MOTHER ABOUT THE FIREWOOD, YOU WOULD'VE DIED.

YOU HAVE TOO MANY GIFTS. THAT SORT OF POWER TENDS TO *BURN OUT* A MORTAL LIFE.

SURE. I DON'T HAVE *ANY* GIFTS.

THAT'S NOT TRUE. YOU CAN BE ANYTHING.

MY MOM USED TO SAY THAT. BUT I *CAN'T* BE ANYTHING. I HAVE *ZERO* SKILLS.

YOU ARE STRETCHED BETWEEN *TWO* WORLDS.

EVEN MORE SO THAN PERCY AND HAZEL.

THE BLOOD OF PYLOS ON YOUR MOTHER'S SIDE, AND YOUR FATHER IS MARS.

NO WONDER JUNO WANTS YOU TO BE ONE OF HER *SEVEN HEROES.*

THE POINT IS, YOU HAVE *OPTIONS*. YOU DON'T NEED TO CONTINUE THIS QUEST. IF YOU DO...I FORESEE YOU DYING WITH THAT FIREWOOD IN YOUR HAND.

I *HAVE* TO GO. IT'S MY JOB.

AND I WON'T EVER ABANDON MY FRIENDS.

I THOUGHT YOU MIGHT SAY THAT. I HAD TO TRY.

BUT IF YOU INSIST ON CONTINUING, I CAN AT LEAST GIVE YOU SOME GUIDANCE.

IN PORTLAND, YOU'LL FIND A BLIND MAN NAMED *PHINEAS*.

HE CAN SEE THE PAST, PRESENT, AND FUTURE. HE KNOWS WHERE THANATOS IS BEING HELD.

BUT BE WARY. PHINEAS HAS A *GRUDGE* AGAINST THE GODS.

AND FIRST, YOU'LL NEED TO CLEAR AWAY THOSE *BASILISKS* OUTSIDE.

IF YOUR FRIENDS TRY... I FORESEE BAD THINGS HAPPENING.

ONLY *YOU* HAVE THE ABILITY TO KILL THE MONSTERS.

"ONLY *YOU* HAVE THE ABILITY TO KILL THE MONSTERS." WOULD'VE BEEN NICE IF SHE'D TOLD ME WHAT THAT ABILITY *IS*.

SOME KID OF THE *WAR GOD* I AM.

NEVER EVEN USED A STUPID *SPEAR*.

NICE SNAKE... NICE, POISONOUS, *ACID-BREATHING* MONSTER SNAKE...

HSsSS

UH-OH.

WHY ARE YOU SO *HEAVY* ALL OF A SUDDEN, SPEAR? GIMME A BREAK, WILL YOU?

CRACK

WELL, *THAT'S* NOT THE BREAK I WAS ASKING FOR.

KREEE!

SHOOMP

WAAGH!

KRIK

THREE CHARGES...

...GUESS THAT LEAVES ME WITH TWO MORE.

FRANK! ARE YOU NUTS?

IRIS SAID YOU CAME OUT TO FIGHT THE *BASILISKS!*

DID YOU... DID YOU ALREADY KILL THEM?

BY *YOURSELF?*

I'LL TELL YOU ABOUT IT LATER.

RIGHT NOW, THERE'S A *BLIND MAN* IN PORTLAND WE'VE GOT TO SEE.

YOUR FRIENDS WILL *DIE*, YES.

BUT I WILL PRESERVE YOU... FOR NOW.

I HAVE *GREAT PLANS* FOR YOU.

WE AWAIT YOU. WHILE YOU FUMBLE YOUR WAY NORTH IN SEARCH OF ME, MY ARMIES WILL DESTROY YOUR PRECIOUS CAMPS.

FIRST THE ROMANS. THEN THE OTHERS.

YOU CANNOT WIN, LITTLE DEMIGOD.

HEH HA HAHAHA!

:GROAN:

GUESS YOU NEEDED TO SLEEP OFF WHATEVER CONCOCTION IRIS GAVE YOU.

YOU WERE OUT *FOREVER*.

FEELING BETTER?

A LITTLE. IT WAS POLYBOTES THAT MADE ME SICK.

GAEA BRED HIM TO KILL NEPTUNE, SO I GUESS THAT MAKES ME *ALLERGIC* TO HIM OR SOMETHING.

I COULDN'T EVEN SEND AN IRIS-MESSAGE LIKE I WANTED.

FLEECY SAID BETWEEN MY AMNESIA AND THE POLYBOTES EFFECT, I COULDN'T MAKE A MENTAL CONNECTION.

WAIT...

WHERE ARE WE?

WELCOME TO PORTLAND. LIKE FRANK SAID, YOU WERE ASLEEP FOR A WHILE.

LUCKILY, THERE WAS A *KILLER WHALE* AND A COUPLE OF *STURGEONS* WHO WERE HAPPY TO HELP THE SEA KING'S SON. THEY TOWED US IN.

I HOPE YOU'RE RESTED.

I DON'T KNOW ABOUT YOU ALL--

"--BUT I COULD USE SOMETHING TO EAT."

WHAT'S A KOREAN/BRAZILIAN FUSION TACO?

NO IDEA. BUT I'LL TAKE TWO.

HAHA! TAKE *THAT*, STUPID BIRDS!

GUYS, IS IT JUST ME--

"--OR ARE THOSE NOT BIRDS?"

WHRRRR

JUST TRY AND EAT! I *DARE* YOU!

AWK!

BACK! BACK!

WHRRNN

UM, CAN WE HELP YOU?

AWK! AWK!

THANK YOU, STRANGERS! YOUR AID IS APPRECIATED!

MY NAME IS *PHINEAS*. IT'S GOOD TO MEET YOU, PERCY, FRANK, AND HAZEL.

HAVE WE MET BEFORE?

OF COURSE NOT. BUT I KNEW WE WOULD.

I'M A *SEER*, AFTER ALL. BLINDNESS NOTWITHSTANDING.

ANYWAY, WE NEED INFORMATION. WE WERE TOLD--

IF YOU HELPED ME, I'D HELP YOU. YES, YES.

BUT YOU'LL HAVE TO DO MORE THAN SCARE AWAY A FEW *HARPIES*.

WE WEREN'T TRYING TO SCARE THEM AWAY.

YOU HAVE PLENTY OF FOOD ON YOUR TABLE.

MAYBE IF YOU *SHARED* SOME. I THINK THEY'RE JUST HUNGRY.

THEY'RE *STARVING!* THAT'S THE POINT!

A LONG TIME AGO, JUPITER CURSED ME AND SENT HARPIES TO STEAL MY FOOD. SEE, I HAD A BIT OF A *BIG MOUTH* AND GAVE AWAY TOO MANY SECRETS.

FOR INSTANCE, HAZEL THERE IS SUPPOSED TO BE *DEAD*.

AND FRANK? YOUR LIFE DEPENDS ON A *BURNT STICK*.

AND PERCY, YOU DON'T REMEMBER WHO YOU ARE AT *ALL!*

SO I EVENTUALLY DIED, AS NOT EATING FOR A *REALLY* LONG TIME WILL DO TO YOU. BUT WHEN MY *PATRON* BROUGHT ME BACK, SHE FLIPPED THINGS.

NOW IT'S THE *HARPIES* THAT GET TO STARVE.

THEY CAN ONLY EAT FROM THIS TABLE, WHICH ME AND MY *WEED WHACKER* WILL NEVER LET THEM DO. *FUN!*

YOUR PATRON?

DON'T PLAY DUMB.

YOU KNOW IT'S *GAEA.* SAME AS YOURS.

HAZEL? WHAT'S HE TALKING ABOUT?

HE'S *AWFUL!* HE BELONGS IN THE FIELDS OF PUNISHMENT!

ONE FORMERLY DEAD PERSON TO ANOTHER? I WOULDN'T BE TALKING.

YOU *STARTED* THIS WHOLE THING. IF IT WEREN'T FOR YOU, ALCYONEUS WOULDN'T BE ALIVE!

THAT'S ENOUGH *LIES.* I'M SHOVING THAT WEED WHACKER UP HIS--

FRANK, WAIT.

PHINEAS, JUST GIVE US A *FAVOR* WE CAN DO FOR YOU, SO YOU CAN TELL US WHERE *THANATOS* IS BEING HELD. THEN WE'LL BE OUT OF YOUR, ER, HAIR.

A FAVOR! YES!

THERE'S THIS *ONE* HARPY. ALWAYS DOES HER OWN THING. WON'T ROOST WITH THE OTHERS. CAN'T VERY WELL *TORMENT* HER IF SHE ISN'T HERE, CAN I?

I'LL TELL YOU ANYTHING YOU WANT TO KNOW.

JUST BRING THAT WRETCHED HARPY TO *ME.*

THERE HAS TO BE A WAY TO GET TO THE ROOF...

BOOKS AND ARCHITECTURE. ANNABETH WOULD LOVE THIS PLACE.

OHHH...

PERCY?

I'M ALL RIGHT. IT'S JUST... ALL THE MISSING MEMORIES.

COME ON. LOOKS LIKE THE STAIRS ARE THIS WAY.

HERE, HARPY, HARPY, HARPY...

OVER THERE.

AWK! ELLA DOESN'T LIKE PHINEAS.

NOPE, NOPE!

ELLA? IS THAT YOUR NAME?

DON'T BE SCARED, ELLA. WE WANT TO BE YOUR FRIENDS.

FRIENDS. TEN SEASONS. 1994 TO 2004.

A HALF-BLOOD OF THE ELDEST GODS, SHALL REACH SIXTEEN AGAINST ALL ODDS.

SIXTEEN. YOU'RE SIXTEEN. PAGE SIXTEEN, MASTERING THE ART OF FRENCH COOKING. INGREDIENTS: BACON, BUTTER...

THOSE LINES. THE PART ABOUT BEING SIXTEEN... I *KNOW* THOSE LINES. I'VE HEARD THEM BEFORE.

I THINK SHE'S QUOTING BOOKS OR SOMETHING.

ELLA, HAVE YOU READ ALL OF THESE?

MORE. MORE DOWNSTAIRS.

WORDS. WORDS CALM ELLA DOWN. WORDS, WORDS, WORDS.

DO YOU REMEMBER THIS ONE, ELLA? WHAT'S ON PAGE SIXTY-TWO, THE THIRD PARAGRAPH?

A HISTORY OF HORSING...

SECRETARIAT. FAVORED THREE TO TWO IN THE 1973 KENTUCKY DERBY, FINISHED AT STANDING TRACK RECORD OF ONE FIFTY-NINE AND TWO-FIFTHS.

SHE'S A *GENIUS*.

AND THEN SOME.

ELLA, WE NEED TO FIGURE OUT A WAY TO BEAT PHINEAS.

AWK! PHINEAS TRIES TO CH-CHAIN ELLA.

HE HURTS ELLA.

PHINEAS IS BAD. MEAN.

ABSOLUTELY. AND WE WON'T LET HIM HURT YOU AGAIN. THAT'S WHY WE NEED TO TRICK HIM.

THINK. DOES HE HAVE ANY *WEAKNESSES*?

CHANCE. GAMES OF CHANCE.

PHINEAS SEES BIG THINGS. PROPHECIES. FATES. GOD STUFF.

NOT SMALL STUFF. RANDOM. EXCITING.

ANY IDEA WHAT SHE MEANS?

I THINK SHE'S SAYING PHINEAS SEES IMPORTANT EVENTS, BUT HE CAN'T SEE SMALL THINGS--LIKE RANDOM ACTS OR SPONTANEOUS GAMES OF CHANCE.

WE NEED TO TEMPT HIM INTO MAKING A *BET*. SOMETHING WITH BIG STAKES HE CAN'T REFUSE.

PHINEAS IS BLIND. GAEA WON'T HEAL. NOPE, NOPE. KEEPS PHINEAS DEPENDENT ON GAEA. YEP.

GORGON'S BLOOD!

WHAT?

ELLA FIGURED IT OUT. UNLESS WE DIE.

DON'T WORRY ABOUT THAT.

"I'VE GOT AN IDEA."

AH! BACK ALREADY.

I HEAR THE FLUTTER OF *NERVOUS* LITTLE WINGS.

I HOPE THAT MEANS YOU'VE BROUGHT MY HARPY.

SHE'S HERE, PHINEAS. BUT SHE'S NOT YOURS. THIS IS BETWEEN YOU AND ME.

A *GAMBLE.*

WINNER GETS WHAT THEY WANT.

FOR ME, THAT MEANS INFORMATION. FOR YOU, THAT MEANS *EYESIGHT.*

OH. AND LOSER DIES.

A GAMBLE? LET ME GUESS-- A SWORD FIGHT. THAT'D BE JUST LIKE A DEMIGOD, CHALLENGING A *BLIND MAN* TO A *DUEL.*

GORGON'S BLOOD. TWO VIALS. ONE HEALS, ONE KILLS. PROBLEM IS, WE DON'T KNOW WHICH IS WHICH. SO IT'S FIFTY-FIFTY. YOU IN?

≥HMPH≤ YOU SAY YOU DON'T KNOW WHICH IS WHICH.

WHY SHOULD I BELIEVE YOU?

BECAUSE I SWEAR AN OATH ON THE RIVER STYX. I BREAK THAT... WELL, THERE ARE *WORSE* THINGS THAN DEATH.

YOU'RE GOING TO WRITE DOWN THE LOCATION OF THANATOS AND SWEAR THE SAME OATH THAT IT'S TRUE. THEN YOU PUT IT IN YOUR POCKET.

I DIE, YOU GET YOUR EYESIGHT BACK.

YOU DIE, I TAKE THE LOCATION FROM YOUR *CORPSE.*

PHINEAS WAS RIGHT WHEN HE SAID I'M SUPPOSED TO BE DEAD.

I'M AN *ESCAPEE* FROM THE UNDERWORLD. I SHOULDN'T BE ALIVE.

IT WAS NEW ORLEANS. *SEVENTY YEARS* AGO. MY MOTHER FELL IN LOVE WITH PLUTO AND WISHED FOR ALL THE RICHES IN THE EARTH. I WAS BORN...CURSED.

GEMS AND PRECIOUS METALS WOULD POP UP WHEREVER I WENT. BUT WHOEVER TRIED TO POSSESS THEM, *TERRIBLE* THINGS HAPPENED TO THEM.

SO WE FLED TO *ALASKA*. MY MOTHER FELL UNDER GAEA'S POWER. SHE MADE MY MOTHER USE ME TO HELP RAISE ALCYONEUS. BUT I WOULDN'T FINISH IT.

I SANK THE ISLAND INTO THE SEA. WE ALL DIED.

I'M A *FAKE*. I ACT LIKE A HERO, BUT I'M BAD. THE THINGS I'VE DONE...

YOU *ARE* A HERO. YOU SACRIFICED YOURSELF TO STOP THE GIANT FROM WAKING. I COULD NEVER BE THAT BRAVE.

HAZEL? WHAT HAPPENED IN THE UNDERWORLD? I MEAN...AFTER YOU DIED. YOU SHOULD'VE GONE TO ELYSIUM.

PLEASE. DON'T ASK ME THAT.

WHY? WHAT'S WRONG?

"SLIP SLIDIN' AWAY." NUMBER FIVE U.S. SINGLE. PAUL SIMON.

SIMON SAYS, GO WITH HER, FRANK.

HAZEL!

HEELLNNN

--TO GO...?

YOU AREN'T *BOTH* GOING TO START BLACKING OUT ON ME NOW, ARE YOU?

NO MORE BLACKOUTS. NOPE, NOPE, NOPE.

I THINK SHE'S RIGHT. I'VE BEEN THROUGH MY ENTIRE PREVIOUS LIFE NOW. ALL THE WAY UP THROUGH MY TIME IN THE UNDERWORLD. PLUS, I FEEL DIFFERENT.

LIKE HAVING FRANK THERE THIS LAST TIME *GROUNDED* ME SOMEHOW.

WASN'T THE SUN OVER THERE? AND WHY ARE WE IN *SEATTLE*?

I PROMISED REYNA I'D DO SOMETHING FOR HER. FIND HER SISTER.

REYNA HAS A *SISTER*?

YEAH. AND REYNA THINKS HER SISTER CAN HELP HER AT CAMP.

BUT SEATTLE IS A BIG PLACE, AND I HAVE NO IDEA WHERE TO LOOK.

AMAZON. LEADING ONLINE RETAILER.

AMAZON.

"CORPORATE HEADQUARTERS IN SEATTLE, WASHINGTON."

YOU DON'T THINK...?

ELLA SEEMS TO KNOW A LOT OF STUFF.

MAY I HELP YOU?

WE'RE LOOKING FOR AMAZONS.

ER, *HYLLA*. WE'RE LOOKING FOR A GIRL NAMED *HYLLA*.

I SEE...

KiNZiE

OTRERA, YOU ARE HERE AS A **GUEST**.

YOU ARE **NOT** QUEEN ANYMORE.

AS YOU SAY-- AT LEAST, UNTIL **TONIGHT**.

BUT I SPEAK THE **TRUTH**. I'VE BEEN BROUGHT BACK BY **GAEA** HERSELF. I BRING TIDINGS OF A NEW WAR.

WHY SHOULD AMAZONS FOLLOW JUPITER, THAT FOOLISH **KING**, WHEN WE CAN FOLLOW A **QUEEN** WHEN I TAKE COMMAND--

IF YOU TAKE COMMAND. FOR NOW, **MY** WORD IS LAW.

AND YOU ARF **DISMISSED**.

TONIGHT, HYLLA.

MY QUEEN? WE HAVE UNINVITED VISITORS.

WHO'D BE MISGUIDED ENOUGH TO--

YOU!

YOU WERE INCREDIBLY FOOLISH TO COME HERE, EVEN FOR A MALE. YOU DESTROYED MY HOME. MADE MY SISTER AND ME EXILES.

CIRCE'S ISLAND, RIGHT?

MAYBE THE GORGON'S BLOOD IS STARTING TO HEAL MY MIND, BECAUSE I REMEMBER NOW.

THE SEA OF MONSTERS. YOU WORKED FOR THE SORCERESS.

YOU SET PIRATES UPON US.

MY SISTER AND I WERE PRISONERS, UNTIL WE FOUGHT OUR WAY OUT. YOU--

WHERE... WHERE DID YOU GET THIS RING?

QUEEN, IF I MAY. YOUR SISTER SENT US TO FIND YOU. CAMP JUPITER IS ABOUT TO BE *BESIEGED*. REYNA NEEDS REINFORCEMENTS. SUPPLIES.

AND YOU'RE SITTING ON A *WEAPONS DEPOT*.

THE ITEMS WE WAREHOUSE HERE ARE FOR OUR FELLOW *AMAZONS* AROUND THE WORLD. IT TOOK MANY YEARS AND MOST OF OUR FORTUNE TO AMASS THIS.

THE ONLY HARMONIOUS SOCIETY IS ONE RULED BY US. SOON, THE *REVOLUTION* WILL BEGIN.

YOUR SISTER MAY NOT BE AN AMAZON, BUT SHE'S STILL YOUR SISTER.

YOU'RE JUST GOING TO *TURN* YOUR *BACK* ON HER?

HEY!

SNAP!

TAKE THE *MALES* TO THE HOLDING CELLS.

THE FEMALE WILL COME WITH ME.

I BELIEVE YOU COME IN PEACE. I BELIEVE REYNA SENT PERCY.

BUT YOU WON'T HELP?

IT'S COMPLICATED. AMAZONS HAVE ALWAYS HAD A ROCKY RELATIONSHIP WITH *DEMIGODS*. ESPECIALLY MALE ONES.

WE FOUGHT FOR KING PRIAM IN THE TROJAN WAR, BUT ACHILLES KILLED OUR QUEEN, PENTHESILEA.

LONG BEFORE THAT, AT THE VERY BEGINNING OF THE AMAZON NATION, A HERO NAMED BELLEROPHON KILLED OUR FIRST QUEEN. *OTRERA*.

YOU MEAN THE LADY WHO--

--WAS HERE BEFORE, YES. THAT WAS OTRERA. OUR FIRST QUEEN. DAUGHTER OF *ARES*.

GAEA BROUGHT HER BACK FROM THE DEAD TO THROW YOU AMAZONS INTO A *CIVIL WAR*.

IF THAT WAS HER PLAN, IT IS WORKING. OTRERA IS A *LEGEND* AMONG OUR PEOPLE.

SHE PLANS TO TAKE BACK THE THRONE AND LEAD US TO *WAR* AGAINST THE ROMANS. MANY OF OUR SISTERS WILL FOLLOW HER.

I MAY NOT BE QUEEN FOR LONG ENOUGH TO SEE.

OTRERA HAS CHALLENGED ME TO A DUEL, AS IS HER *RIGHT* AS AN AMAZON.

TONIGHT, WE'LL BATTLE FOR THE *THRONE*. TO THE DEATH.

I *WARN* YOU: THE LAST GIRL WHO TRIED TO TOUCH ARION NOW HAS A *METAL ARM.*

OH, HE ISN'T SO BAD. ARE YOU, ARION?

MAYBE HE CAN SMELL GOLD ON ME. SUMMONING PRECIOUS STONES AND METALS FROM UNDERGROUND IS KIND OF MY THING.

WE SPENT YEARS HUNTING FOR THIS HORSE.

IT WAS FORETOLD THAT THE MOST *COURAGEOUS* FEMALE WARRIOR WOULD SOMEDAY MASTER ARION AND RIDE HIM TO VICTORY. THAT THERE WOULD BE A NEW ERA OF PROSPERITY FOR THE AMAZONS.

YET HE'LL LET NO AMAZON TOUCH HIM, MUCH LESS *CONTROL* HIM.

PERHAPS...

HAZEL, OTRERA'S FOLLOWERS WILL BE ON SHIFT GUARDING THE CELLS WHERE YOUR FRIENDS ARE BEING KEPT.

IT WOULD WEAKEN HER STANDING IF HER FOLLOWERS FAILED IN THEIR DUTIES.

IF, FOR EXAMPLE, THEY WERE OVERCOME BY AN OUTSIDER AND *A PRISON BREAK* OCCURRED.

OF COURSE, NONE OF YOUR FOLLOWERS WOULD KNOW ANYTHING ABOUT IT.

NOT A THING. NOT EVEN IF YOU AND YOUR FRIENDS MADE IT BACK HERE AND USED ARION TO ESCAPE.

IF ARION WAS UNGUARDED, AND YOU ENCOUNTERED NO RESISTANCE FROM ANY LOYAL TO ME--THAT WOULD BE A *COMPLETE* COINCIDENCE.

AND IF WE SUCCEED IN OUR QUEST AND FREE THANATOS, THEN OTRERA WON'T BE ABLE TO COME BACK FROM THE DEAD ANYMORE.

A *TRAGEDY*.

AH, BUT WHAT USE ARE HYPOTHETICALS? I AM QUEEN OF THE AMAZONS. I WOULD *NEVER* AID IN THE ESCAPE OF DEMIGOD PRISONERS.

ESPECIALLY MALE ONES.

AND THIS CONVERSATION *NEVER* HAPPENED.

YOU! HOW DID YOU GET HERE UNESCORTED?

TWO BATTLE-HARDENED AMAZONS AGAINST JUST ME.

IT HARDLY SEEMS FAIR--

--FOR YOU.

GET CLEAR!

KRAKOOM

SHINK

HAZEL! THAT WAS AWESOME!

TAKING A CHILD OF PLUTO INTO AN *UNDERGROUND* CAVERN PROBABLY WASN'T THE SMARTEST THING FOR THEM TO DO.

OW!

WE DON'T HAVE MUCH TIME! FOLLOW ME!

THIS *FUTILE* ESCAPE ATTEMPT HAS GONE ON QUITE *LONG* ENOUGH!

READY TO STRETCH YOUR LEGS, BOY?

BRRRRFFFT

YAH!

CRASH!

AAAAAAAA!

FIVE MINUTES AND FIFTY MILES LATER.

THAT WAS *FUN!*

YEAH.

SLURP!

SO MUCH FUN.

YOU HUNGRY, ARION?

I DON'T SENSE ANY GOLD UNDERGROUND HERE, SO WHY DON'T YOU GO FIND A PLACE TO--

--GRAZE.

HEY...THIS IS LYNN CANYON PARK.

I'M PRACTICALLY *HOME.* MY GRANDMOTHER'S HOUSE IS A SHORT WALK FROM HERE.

I KNOW THIS AREA LIKE THE BACK OF MY--

HUP!

THOK

THOK

THOK

HRN?

OW--

FOOMP

RIB BONES FOR BOOMERANGS. SWEET.

TOO BAD THAT WAS THE *EASY* PART.

WE HAVE TO SNEAK DOWN TO THE HOUSE. GRANDMOTHER IS IN A *WORLD* OF *TROUBLE*.

WASN'T ME, KID. I ALWAYS LIKED THE OLD BIRD.

THE DECISION IS HERS. SHE'S READY TO DIE. BEEN READY FOR WEEKS, BUT SHE WAS HOLDING OUT FOR YOU.

FOR ME? HOW COULD SHE KNOW I WAS COMING BACK? *I* DIDN'T KNOW.

THE LAISTRYGONIANS OUTSIDE KNEW.

I IMAGINE GAEA TOLD THEM. SHE'S BEEN KEEPING TABS ON YOU.

YOU WORRY HER MORE THAN PERCY OR JASON OR ANY OF THE OTHER SEVEN.

THE SEVEN...

YOU MEAN IN THE ANCIENT PROPHECY, THE DOORS OF DEATH. *I'M* ONE OF THE SEVEN, AND JASON, AND--

BINGO. JUNO'S BIG PLAN IS TO *UNITE* THE GREEKS AND THE ROMANS, AND SIC YOU ON THE GIANTS *TOGETHER*. SHE THINKS THAT'S THE WAY TO BEAT GAEA.

PERCY AND THE OTHERS, GAEA THINKS SHE CAN CONTROL.

BUT *YOU* WORRY HER. SHE'D RATHER JUST KILL YOU FLAT OUT.

NOW THAT YOU'RE HERE, I IMAGINE THE ATTACK WILL COME IN THE MORNING. YOUR SPEAR WON'T BE READY TO USE AGAIN FOR A WHILE, SO I HOPE YOU'VE LEARNED HOW TO USE THE *FAMILY GIFT*.

OR YOU AND YOUR PALS WILL BE *BREAKFAST* FOR CANNIBALS.

THE FAMILY GIFT...

IS THAT WHAT SHE WANTS TO TELL ME?

WHEN SHE WAKES UP, SHE'LL GIVE YOU SOME HELP. THEN SHE'LL PROBABLY DIE.

WHAT? I HAVE TO SAVE HER!

SHE'S READY TO MOVE ON. LIFE IS ONLY PRECIOUS BECAUSE IT *ENDS*, KID.

TAKE IT FROM A GOD. YOU MORTALS DON'T KNOW HOW LUCKY YOU ARE.

LUCKY? *YOUR* MOM'S STILL ALIVE. SO DON'T TELL ME ABOUT LUCKY. ALL YOU AND YOUR STUPID *WARS* DO IS TAKE PEOPLE AWAY.

SELF-PITY ISN'T WORTHY OF YOU, KID. YOUR MOM GAVE YOU ALL HER BEST TRAITS--BRAVERY, LOYALTY, BRAINS. FIGURE OUT HOW TO *USE* THEM.

YOU CAN STILL FREE THANATOS AND SAVE THE CAMP.

WAR IS DUTY. THE ONLY REAL CHOICE IS WHAT SIDE YOU FIGHT FOR.

THE LEGACY OF ROME IS ON THE LINE--FIVE THOUSAND YEARS OF LAW, ORDER, CIVILIZATION.

IT'S ALL GOING TO *CRUMBLE*. UNLESS YOU *WIN* THIS.

YOU'RE *LATE*, FAI.

GRANDMOTHER, I...

HUSH, YOU SILLY **OX**.

I WAS SOMEWHAT PLEASED WHEN THE OGRES SAID YOU WERE COMING BACK.

THOUGH THEY WISH TO EAT YOU, WHICH IS RIDICULOUS. YOU WOULD TASTE TERRIBLE.

I HAVE MADE PREPARATIONS. INSIDE MY NIGHTSTAND, YOU WILL FIND THE DETAILS OF YOUR ESCAPE PLAN.

THERE IS A PILOT WAITING FOR YOU AT THE AIRFIELD NORTH OF THE ESTATE.

HE'S AN OLD FAMILY FRIEND. GIVE HIM THE ENVELOPE.

BUT WHAT ABOUT--

DO NOT WORRY ABOUT ME, BOY. MARS TOLD ME OF YOUR QUEST. FULFILL YOUR DUTY AND RECLAIM THE FAMILY'S HONOR.

YOU'LL DIE. I...I'LL NEVER SEE YOU AGAIN.

I WILL DIE ANYWAY. I'M **OLD**. NOW ABOUT YOUR POWERS. YOU **HAVE** FIGURED THEM OUT...?

UH...

GODS OF YOUR ANCESTORS, BOY! HAVE YOU LEARNED **NOTHING**?

WHAT DID YOUR MOTHER ALWAYS TELL YOU?

"YOU CAN BE ANYTHING."

FINALLY, A DIM LIGHT GOES ON IN THAT HEAD OF YOURS. YOUR MOTHER WAS NOT SIMPLY BOOSTING YOUR SELF-ESTEEM. SHE WAS TELLING YOU THE *LITERAL* TRUTH.

BUT... *ANYTHING?*

WITHIN REASON. LIVING THINGS. *CREATURES.* YOU CAN'T BE A POTTED PLANT.

THOUGH, GODS KNOW, YOU SURE SEEM TO TRY.

WHY DO YOU LOOK SO SURPRISED?

YOU HAVE ALWAYS SAID YOU ARE NOT COMFORTABLE IN YOUR OWN BODY.

ALL OF US WITH THE BLOOD OF PYLOS FEEL THAT WAY.

THIS GIFT WAS ONLY GIVEN *ONCE* TO A MORTAL FAMILY.

WE ARE UNIQUE AMONG DEMIGODS.

YOU MUST GO. *SLEEP.* REGAIN YOUR STRENGTH BEFORE THE OGRES ATTACK. I HAVE SAID ALL I NEED TO. THERE ARE PREPARATIONS FOR MYSELF TO MAKE.

LET ME STAY! I WON'T LET THEM GET YOU.

~pfft~

I WILL DIE IN MY *OWN* WAY. AND IT WILL NOT BE GNASHED BETWEEN THE TEETH OF AN OGRE.

NOW GO!

...THANK YOU, GRANDMOTHER.

I'LL MAKE YOU PROUD.

YES, FAI. YOU *WILL*.

GRANDMOTHER?

BWOOOSH

WHOA!

COME AND GET IT, BOYS!

KLING KLING KLING

KISS THE COOK

HERO IS ON THE MENU!

WE HAVE TO *FIGHT!* WHERE'S FRANK?

GARAGE! CADILLAC!

WHY ARE YOU IN THE BACK?

I DON'T EVEN HAVE A *LEARNER'S PERMIT!*

DO YOU KNOW HOW TO DRIVE?

GUYS, THERE'S SOMETHING I HAVE TO TELL YOU.

WHATEVER IT IS, IT CAN WAIT. YOU NEED TO MOURN.

NO. IT'S IMPORTANT. FOR *ALL* OF US. SOMETHING MARS TOLD ME.

YOU SAW *MARS*?

UNFORTUNATELY.

HE SAYS TO DEFEAT GAEA, JUNO WANTS ME TO BRING DEMIGODS TOGETHER. ROMAN-- AND *GREEK*.

THEN IT'S TRUE. THERE *IS* ANOTHER CAMP. THAT *HAS* TO BE WHERE I CAME FROM.

IF OCTAVIAN FINDS OUT, HE'LL START A *WAR*.

HE'S ALWAYS BELIEVED THE GREEKS WERE OUT THERE PLOTTING AGAINST US.

IF IT'S TRUE-- IF YOU *ARE* FROM A GREEK CAMP-- WHAT DO WE DO?

I DON'T KNOW...BUT I HAD A DREAM WHERE I SAW ANOTHER CAMP BUILDING A FLYING SHIP TO FIGHT GAEA.

IF THEY SHOW UP AT CAMP JUPITER UNANNOUNCED...

I HAVE TO WARN THEM SOMEHOW.

MAYBE MY DREAMS CAN SEND INFORMATION BACK THEIR WAY. THEY CAN HELP ELLA, TOO.

WILL THAT WORK? TALKING THROUGH YOUR DREAMS?

I'M NOT SURE.

"BUT I HAVE TO TRY."

-snnrt-

RRRCH

WELCOME TO ALASKA. WE'RE OFFICIALLY BEYOND THE HELP OF THE GODS.

HOW FAR TO THE HUBBARD GLACIER? I SAW *POLYBOTES'S ARMY* IN MY DREAM. THEY'VE ALMOST REACHED CAMP.

WE'RE HERE AT THE AIRFIELD IN SEWARD. THE GLACIER IS EAST OF US, HERE.

THE EASIEST WAY IS BY BOAT, BUT IT'S STILL OVER *THREE HUNDRED* MILES.

GEE, IS THAT ALL?

WE BETTER GET MOVING.

"THERE'S A PLACE WHERE WE CAN REST ALONG THE WAY."

THIS IS YOUR OLD HOUSE? WHERE YOU AND YOUR MOM--

YES. THIS IS THE PLACE.

I SLEPT RIGHT OVER HERE.

THESE...THESE ARE MY OLD KEEPSAKES. I CAN'T BELIEVE THEY'RE STILL HERE...

WHO IS HE? HE LOOKS FAMILIAR.

YOU DON'T KNOW HIM. HE WAS A FRIEND OF MINE IN NEW ORLEANS.

AFTER I MOVED HERE, I NEVER SAW HIM AGAIN. HE'S BEEN DEAD OVER FORTY YEARS.

ARE YOU *SURE*? I COULD SWEAR--

THANATOS! WE'RE HERE TO **RESCUE** YOU! CALL OFF THE SHADES!

RESCUE ME?

DO YOU UNDERSTAND WHAT YOU ARE SAYING, HAZEL LEVESQUE?

DAUGHTER OF PLUTO, CHILD OF MY MASTER, YOU OF **ALL** PEOPLE SHOULD NOT WISH ME RELEASED.

LISTEN, DEATH. I DIDN'T COME BACK FROM THE UNDERWORLD AND TRAVEL **THOUSANDS** OF MILES TO BE TOLD THAT I'M **STUPID** FOR SETTING YOU FREE.

IF I DIE, I DIE. I'LL FIGHT THIS WHOLE **ARMY** IF I HAVE TO.

JUST TELL ME HOW TO BREAK YOUR CHAINS.

INTERESTING. YOU DO UNDERSTAND THE SHADES WERE ONCE *DEMIGODS*, LIKE YOU?

THEY FOUGHT FOR ROME. THEY DIED WITHOUT COMPLETING THEIR HEROIC QUESTS AND WERE SENT TO ASPHODEL.

NOW GAEA HAS PROMISED THEM A *SECOND* LIFE IF THEY FIGHT FOR HER. I DO NOT CONTROL THEM. THE *GIANT* DOES.

WE'RE WASTING TIME.

SHNNK

THAT WILL NOT WORK. ONLY THE *FIRE* OF *LIFE* CAN MELT THE CHAINS OF DEATH.

WE DON'T HAVE TIME FOR RIDDLES!

IT ISN'T A RIDDLE...

WELCOME!

HAZEL. THAT PACKAGE YOU'RE KEEPING FOR ME? I NEED IT.

FRANK, NO.

THERE HAS TO BE *ANOTHER* WAY.

PLEASE. I...I KNOW WHAT I'M DOING.

ONLY THE FIRE OF LIFE CAN MELT THE CHAINS OF DEATH.

YOU'RE RIGHT, FRANK ZHANG. *SACRIFICES* MUST BE MADE.

FREE!

GREAT. NOW *DO SOMETHING!*

I WILL WATCH. THOSE WHO DIE IN BATTLE WILL STAY DEAD.

HOW'S THAT?

I WAS HOPING FOR SOMETHING A LITTLE MORE *PROACTIVE!*

HOW IS MY AIM *NOW*, GIRL?

AAAA!

WHAMM

GRAWWWR!

SMAK

RARRGH!

THAT'S FAR ENOUGH!

I'VE NEVER KNOWN A CHILD OF MARS WHO CAN CHANGE HIS FORM...

...BUT THAT DOESN'T MEAN YOU CAN DEFEAT ME.

DO YOU THINK YOUR *STUPID* SOLDIER OF A FATHER GAVE YOU THE **STRENGTH** TO FACE ME IN COMBAT?

YOU KNOW WHAT I GOT FROM MY FATHER?

TACTICS. A BATTLE CAN BE WON *BEFORE* IT'S EVER FOUGHT BY CHOOSING THE RIGHT GROUND.

CAN YOU FEEL IT? WE AREN'T IN ALASKA ANYMORE.

YOUR HOMELAND IS ABOUT A HUNDRED YARDS *THAT* WAY.

I'LL--I'LL--

GAH!

BRING IT.

=WOOOFF=

=URGGL=

MAY I?

BY ALL MEANS.

WELCOME TO *CANADA,* IDIOT.

KRENNCH

WHAT HAPPENED?

I HAPPENED.

WE'RE WITHIN SPITTING DISTANCE OF THE PACIFIC.

ONCE YOU ALL WERE SAFELY *NOT HERE*, I CUT LOOSE. BYE-BYE, CAMP TUNDRA.

THE GHOSTS?

DROWNED AND PROBABLY BACK IN THE *UNDERWORLD* BY NOW.

I GATHERED ALL THEIR WEAPONS, THOUGH. FIGURED WE COULD USE THEM.

SO, YOU CAN TURN INTO A *BEAR*.

AND AN ELEPHANT.

AND AN *ELEPHANT*?

THAT'S THE FAMILY GIFT MY GRANDMOTHER WAS TRYING TO TELL ME ABOUT.

WHO KNEW?

IF YOU GUYS ARE DONE CHATTING, IT'S TIME TO *GO*. CAMP JUPITER IS UNDER ATTACK, AND THEY CAN USE THAT EAGLE.

THE AMAZONS SAID YOU EAT GOLD, ARION.

HERE'S SOME *HIGH-PERFORMANCE* FUEL. *IMPERIAL* GOLD.

CHOMP

HOW FAST YOU THINK YOU CAN GET US TO CAMP?

OH *YEAH!*

AAAAAAAA!

FBOOM

AAAIGH!

GYAAA!

THE ONE WHO *KILLS* THE MOST GETS THE MOST *SNACKS!*

OH, NO...

WE'RE TOO LATE.

IT'S A *SLAUGHTER.*

BROTHER!

CYCLOPS! LOOK OUT!

BROTHER! BROTHER!

HEY, TYSON.

GOOD TO SEE YOU TOO, BIG GUY.

ROOOF!

ELLA! YOU'RE SAFE!

TYSON FOUND ELLA.

TYSON TOOK CARE OF ELLA. *AWWK!*

TAKE IT EASY. THIS IS MY BROTHER, TYSON, AND HIS PET *HELLHOUND,* MRS. O'LEARY.

THEY'RE ON OUR SIDE.

FRANK ZHANG, RECIPIENT OF THE MURAL CROWN. LEAD ON.

I'M SUPPOSED TO TOP *THAT*?

YOU CAN AND WILL.

I'VE GOT A *GIANT* TO KILL.

CHARGE!

GALK!

CUT THEM DOWN!

EEE-IPE!

FIFTH COHORT!

IMPERIAL GOLD WEAPONS! *ARM* YOURSELVES!

BACK OFF, MEAN CYCLOPS, MA'AM!

WHAT IS THIS?

WHAT IS HAPPENING?!

THIS IS US *KICKING* YOUR *TAIL*, FISH BREATH.

YOU. ME. TO THE *FINISH*.

HOLD STILL.

I HOPE THAT *HURT.*

YOU MORE THAN ME, *OCTAVIAN.*

HOW ABOUT OUR *FIFTH COHORT,* EH! BRINGING BACK THE LEGION'S *EAGLE!* LEADING THE *CHARGE* AGAINST POLYBOTES'S ARMY!

I NEVER DOUBTED ANY OF YOU FOR A MOMENT! WE'RE *BACK!* NO MORE *CURSE!*

AS LONG AS YOU'RE HAPPY, VITELLIUS.

OF COURSE I'M HAPPY!

I *KNEW* JACKSON WOULD AMOUNT TO SOMETHING!

A SUCCESSFUL QUEST, PERCY JACKSON.

WELL DONE.

THAT'S ALL YOU HAVE TO SAY TO ME, JUNO?

YOU TOOK AWAY MY MEMORIES. STOLE *EIGHT MONTHS* OF MY LIFE FOR A QUEST THAT TOOK ONLY A *WEEK*.

EIGHT! MONTHS!

YOU WEREN'T NEEDED AT CAMP UNTIL NOW.

TO SAVE THE ROMANS AT THEIR MOMENT OF *GREATEST* CRISIS.

YOU KNOW I'M RIGHT.

AND DURING THOSE EIGHT MONTHS, *JASON GRACE* HAS HAD TIME TO LEARN TO TRUST THE GREEKS.

TOGETHER, YOU AND HE WILL *UNITE* THE CAMPS.

WHY ME?

BECAUSE I KNOW YOU.

YOU ARE *IMPULSIVE*, BUT WHEN IT COMES TO YOUR FRIENDS, YOU ARE AS *CONSTANT* AS A COMPASS NEEDLE.

YOU ARE UNSWERVINGLY LOYAL, AND SO YOU INSPIRE LOYALTY. YOU ARE THE *GLUE* THAT WILL HOLD THE SEVEN TOGETHER.

JUPITER, MY PROUD AND *OBSTINATE* HUSBAND, BELIEVES THE GIANTS CAN BE FOUGHT WITHOUT THE DEMIGODS, AND GAEA CAN BE FORCED BACK TO HER SLUMBERS.

I KNOW BETTER. BUT YOU MUST *PROVE* YOURSELVES.

ONLY BY SAILING TO THE *ANCIENT LANDS* AND CLOSING THE DOORS OF DEATH WILL YOU CONVINCE HIM YOU ARE WORTHY.

AND IF WE FAIL?

IF GREEKS AND ROMANS DON'T GET ALONG, AND WE DON'T CONVINCE THE GODS?

THEN GAEA HAS ALREADY WON.

COURAGE FOR WHAT COMES NEXT, PERCY JACKSON.

YOU ARE HOME SAFE AND VICTORIOUS--

--BUT YOUR *JOURNEY* HAS ONLY JUST BEGUN.

SOMETHING APPROACHES! *SOUND* THE *ALARM!*

THEY MADE IT.

ANNABETH.

PERCY! EVERYONE IS LOOKING FOR YOU!

REYNA ORDERED HIGH ALERT! *BATTLE* FORMATIONS!

ARE YOU *LISTENING?* WE'RE ABOUT TO BE *ATTACKED!*

GUYS, IT'S FINE.

YOU FEEL LIKE TAKING ANOTHER TRIP?

COME ON. I CAN'T LEAVE MY *TEAM* BEHIND.

NOT AFTER ALL THOSE TIMES WE ALMOST GOT OURSELVES KILLED.

"--LET ME INTRODUCE YOU TO MY *OTHER* FAMILY."

3 1901 10095 3795

END.